"Ricky's Dream Trip to Colonial America"

Written by William Stevenson, Ed. D.

Design by

 **Fireman Creative**

Illustration by Nicole Dalton

Published by PopPop Press in association with OffTheBookshelf.com

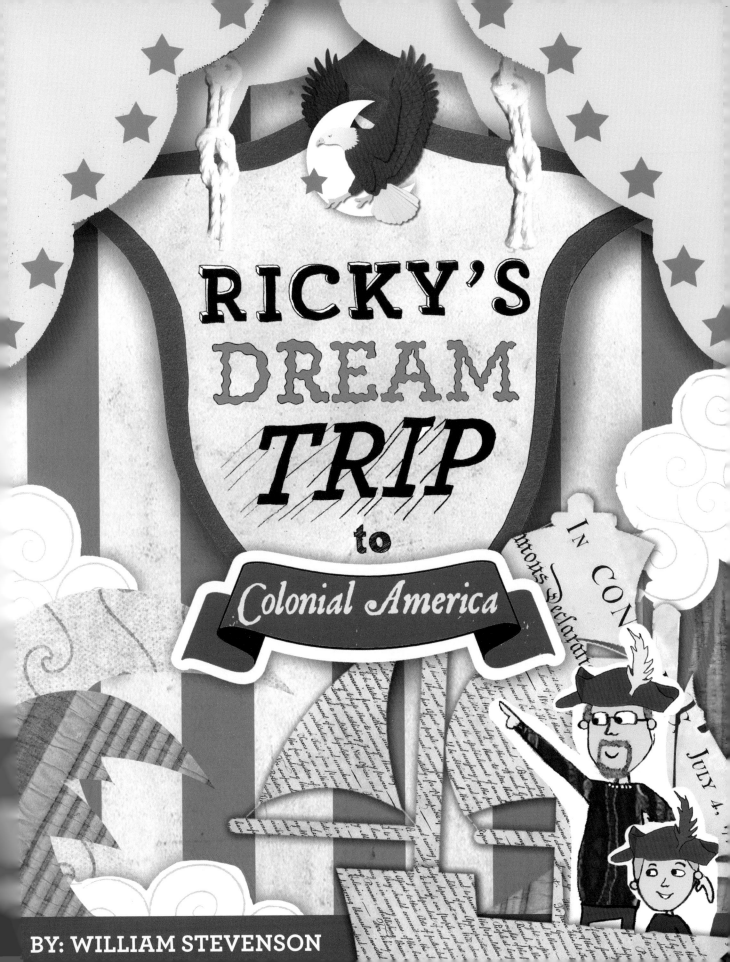

RICKY'S DREAM TRIP to Colonial America

BY: WILLIAM STEVENSON

WORLD'S BEST
POP POP

Ricky is a very smart ten year old boy and he has a rich imagination. In our story Ricky will use his dream imagination to travel back in time to Colonial America with his Pop Pop.

Ricky finished his homework, practiced his guitar lesson, put on his pajamas, hugged his Mommy and Daddy, and went to bed. He was very tired and fell asleep as soon as his head hit the pillow. He dreamed his Pop Pop came into his room.

"Pop Pop, what are you doing here? You and Mom Mom drove home yesterday. Did you come back?"

"I am here because you dreamed me into your room."

"Does Mommy know you're here, Pop Pop?"

"No one knows I am here because I am in your dream. Would you like to go on a secret dream trip with me?"

"I will have to ask Mommy and Daddy."

"This is your dream, Ricky. You can travel anywhere you want to go."

"OK, Pop Pop. Where are we going?"

"If you use your dream imagination, we can travel back in time to Colonial America."

"How can we travel back in time, Pop Pop?"

"In your dreams you can go anywhere. Are you ready to begin our journey?"

"Awesome. Can I bring my guitar?"

"Absolutely. It is your dream."

"Blink your eyes and we'll be dressed in clothing worn by the colonists in 1776. We want to look just like everybody else almost 250 years ago."

"Pop Pop, what is a colonist?"

"A colonist is a person living in Colonial America. Before United States of America was a country, people lived in thirteen separate colonies. Each colony was like its own little country but they were owned by Great Britain and King George III. The word, colonist, comes from colony. Get it?"

"I got it." Ricky blinked. "Pop Pop, you look funny. Ha! Ha! Where did you find those clothes? What kind of pants are you wearing?"

"They are called breeches and all men and boys wore them. If you think I look funny, Ricky, just look in the mirror and see what you dreamed for both of us. Ha! Ha!"

"It looks like we're ready to go but how are we going to get back to the year 1776?"

H.M.S. DREAM

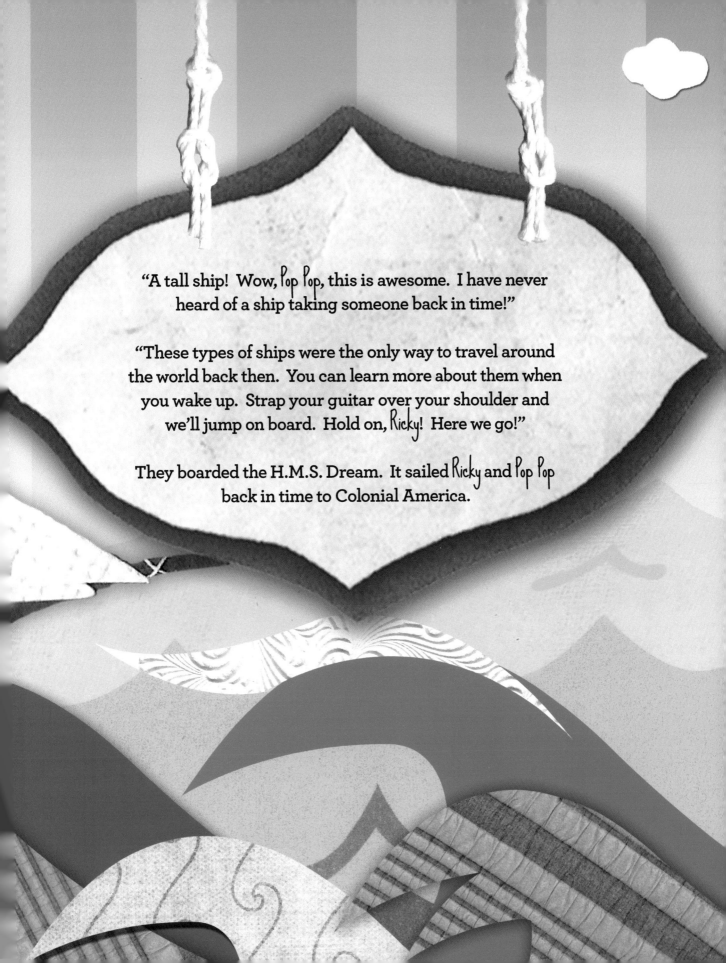

"A tall ship! Wow, Pop Pop, this is awesome. I have never heard of a ship taking someone back in time!"

"These types of ships were the only way to travel around the world back then. You can learn more about them when you wake up. Strap your guitar over your shoulder and we'll jump on board. Hold on, Ricky! Here we go!"

They boarded the H.M.S. Dream. It sailed Ricky and Pop Pop back in time to Colonial America.

"That was fast, Pop Pop. Look at the ship. It is back in water and no longer traveling through time. Now it looks like all the other ships in the harbor. Where are we?"

"The harbor appears foggy so the H.M.S. Dream can quietly land in the water and blend in with all the other ships. We have landed near Independence Hall in Philadelphia on July 1, 1776. Our plan is to go inside Independence Hall to talk with some of the delegates from the thirteen colonies. They are meeting in the Assembly Room."

"Why are they meeting? I don't know what to say to them, Pop Pop. I am very nervous."

"Don't be nervous, Ricky. This is *your* dream."

"The people that are inside the Assembly Room are talking about whether or not the thirteen colonies should vote to be separated from Great Britain. You can ask some of them why they are voting for or against independence."

"Sounds scary to me, but I'll try, Pop Pop. Before we go inside, I'd like to talk to that little boy. Do you see him? He's crying; maybe he's lost."

"Good idea, Ricky. Let's see if we can help him."

"Hi. Why are you crying? Are you lost?"

"No. I'm a slave and my owner is inside. He brought me with him to watch his horse while he is in meetings. I'm sad because I'm not allowed to go to school. The law keeps slaves like me from going to school and learning how to read and write. If I knew how to read, at least my mind would be free."

"That makes me sad. What is your name? My name is Ricky and this is my Pop Pop."

"Kofi. It means I was born on Friday. What is on your back, Master Ricky?"

"Oh, this is my guitar. It is my favorite thing in the whole world. Would you like to hear me play it for you?"

"Yes. I'd really like that."

Ricky played Animal Fair, a very old and famous song.

"Thanks, Ricky. You are a very special boy. I'll never forget you. You treated me like a human being."

"Where I come from there are no slaves and everyone is treated like a human being. In the future, everyone is free. We are going in to Independence Hall. We'll see you before we leave."

"Good-bye, Ricky; good-bye Pop Pop."

"See you, Kofi. Are we ready to go inside, Pop Pop? I am still a little scared, though."

As Ricky and Pop Pop walked in to Independence Hall, a voice boomed out.

"Hey, this is the Continental Congress and we are having a private meeting. You can't come in here. What is your name little boy? I am John Adams."

"I'm Ricky and this is my Pop Pop. My Pop Pop said I could go anywhere in my dreams. Actually, I'm dreaming you and you would not be here without my dream."

"OK, I guess you're right my little Ricky. We are having a secret meeting so everyone can feel free to speak their mind. No one outside the Assembly Room is supposed to hear us argue and we are not allowed to keep notes of what is said. Do you understand, Ricky?"

"Yes, I do, Mr. Adams. Why is it so hot in here? Don't you have air conditioning?"

"We have all the windows closed so no one outside can hear us. I have never heard of air conditioning. Let me introduce you and your Pop Pop. Chairman Harrison and gentlemen, Ricky and his Pop Pop will be joining us on this very historic day. After all, it is his dream.

Now please sit down, Ricky. Mr. John Dickinson is about to speak to us about his opinion on independence."

"Thank you, Mr. Adams. I am asking all of the delegates gathered here today to vote against Thomas Jefferson's declaration that the thirteen colonies should be free and independent states. We must do everything possible to reduce the fever of independence that has infected so many of our citizens."

Ricky stood up. "Mr. Dickinson?"

"Yes, Ricky."

"Why are you against voting for independence from Great Britain? Don't you want to be free?"

"There are many reasons, young man. We have been discussing independence for many, many months.

If we were independent from Great Britain, our Mother country, I fear that the colonies would never join together. I believe they would break up into thirteen separate, weak little countries. We need more time to organize the thirteen colonies into a new country that would be strong and united. Do you understand my fears?"

John Adams rose to speak to the delegates, who numbered about 50 gentlemen.

"How could Ricky understand your scare tactics, Mr. Dickinson?

This ten year old boy is more afraid of the flashing lightning and the loud thunder booming above our heads. Ricky, do you have another question?"

"Mr. Adams, Mr. Dickinson, thunder and lightning do not scare me, either. I am afraid that the Continental Congress is going to make the wrong decision about independence. Why are you going to sign the Declaration of Independence?"

"I am glad that you are worried about our decision. Lots of people of all ages are worried. We have been talking about independence from Great Britain for a long time. Mr. Jefferson struggled for a long time to put down on paper just the right words in which we could agree. He has written a beautiful declaration that will be respected for hundreds of years. When the delegates come to an agreement on all the terms, I will be signing the Declaration of Independence because it will save America."

"Why will America be saved by declaring independence?"

"Good question, Ricky. By signing it, we all will have to agree to defend America. If we don't sign it, we will agree to let Great Britain and King George III rule us."

"But how can we fight against the greatest army in the world?"

"That is a good point, little man. There comes a time in our life when we need to stand up to a bully, even if it is a giant. Freedom is not free. I believe that the right to be free is worth the cost not only with our treasure, but with our lives."

Many delegates stood up and cheered. Several colonies were still against declaring indpendence and their delegates sat quietly.

"My dear Ricky, I have finished my speech and we would like to hear from you. Is there anything that you would like to share with us before we come back tomorrow morning when we will be voting for or against independence?"

"Mr. Adams, I am only ten years old."

"That's true, young man, but what we decide tomorrow will affect all ten year old boys and girls now and in the future."

"Instead of giving a speech, can I play the delegates a song Pop Pop taught me?"

H.M.S. DREAM

"That will be acceptable."

Ricky played his guitar as he and his Pop Pop sang "Blowing in the Wind." When the song was over, the delegates were stunned in silence until John Adams arose from his seat and began clapping. Soon all the delegates were on their feet cheering and yelling Ricky's name. As they left the Assembly Room, Ricky and Pop Pop turned and waived good-bye. Ricky whispered something into John Adams' ear as he shook their hands.

The two visitors from the future left the building.

Ricky and Pop Pop boarded the H.M.S. Dream and sailed off into the foggy sea. Once out of sight, the ship flew through time and soon Ricky and Pop Pop were back home.

"Pop Pop, that was a cool dream. Thank you, but thank you is not enough. Thank you a hundred times over and over."

"Bye, Ricky, I love you."

"I love you, too, Pop Pop."

Ricky woke up. "Mommy, Daddy! Wake up! Pop Pop came into my dream and we ..." Ricky fell back to sleep.

THE END!
Until Next Time...

FUN FACTS

Tricorn Hat

Towards the end of the 17th century the vast wigs then worn by some men made it impractical for them to wear the fashionable broad-brimmed hat unless necessary.

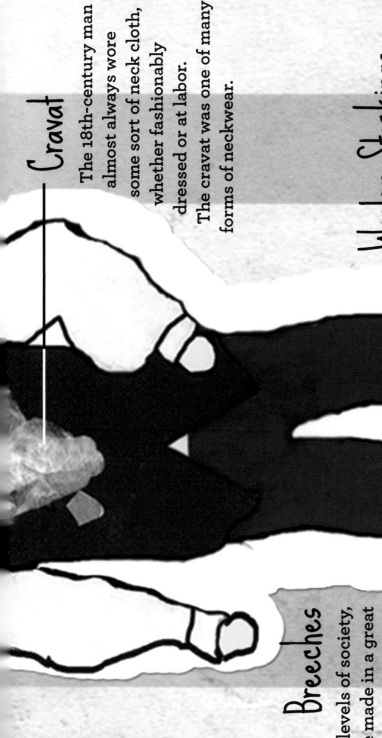

Cravat

The 18th-century man almost always wore some sort of neck cloth, whether fashionably dressed or at labor. The cravat was one of many forms of neckwear.

Woolen Stockings

Stockings of the 18th century were worn by men and women, and were most often knit.

Breeches

Worn by all levels of society, breeches were made in a great variety of silks, cottons, linens, wools, knits, and leathers.

Leather Shoes

Men's shoes were made in a great variety of styles and qualities. Fashionable low-heeled shoes or pumps were of softer leather, coarse common shoes of sturdier leathers.